A My Name Is Alice

An Alphabet Book

by Virginia Holt
illustrated by Joe Mathieu

**Featuring Jim Henson's
Sesame Street Muppets**

A Random House PICTUREBACK®

Random House/Children's Television Workshop

Library of Congress Cataloging-in-Publication Data:
Holt, Virginia. A my name is Alice : a Sesame Street alphabet book / by Virginia Holt. p. cm.–(A Random House pictureback) SUMMARY: The Muppets introduce the alphabet with short poems about dinosaurs, cookies, ladders, quilts, and zebras. ISBN: 0-394-82241-2 (pbk.); 0-394-92241-7 (lib. bdg.) 1. English language–Alphabet–Juvenile literature. 2. Children's poetry, American. [1. Alphabet. 2. American poetry] I. Title. II. Title: Sesame Street alphabet book. III. Series. PE1155.H64 1989 421'.54–dc19 [E] 88-18520

Manufactured in the United States of America   4 5 6 7 8 9 0

Aa

A my name is Alice,
and my brother's Aloysius.
My favorite food is apples,
and I think they are delicious.

Bb

B my name is Bert,
and I love to throw my ball.
I take turns with my buddy
as we bounce it off the wall.

Cc

C my name is Cookie,
and me tell you, chocolate chips
are my very favorite cookies!
Oh, they make me smack my lips!

Dd

D this is a dinosaur
that's called Tyrannosaurus.
He doesn't live here anymore
but left his bones here for us.

TYRANNOSAURUS

Ee

E my name is Ernie,
and this is my little ear.
I bet you have a set yourself.
That's how we both can hear.

Ff

F I found a feather!
It was floating in the air.
Do you think it could belong
to that big bird over there?

Gg

G my name is Grover,
and this white bird is a goose.
I have to run and grab it
if it happens to get loose.

Hh

H my name is Herry,
and this animal's a horse.
I give him lots of hay, yah,
at feeding time, of course.

Ii

I this is an iceberg.
It's an island made of ice.
For me it's kind of chilly
but these penguins think it's nice.

Jj

J my jellybeans are
in a jar high on the shelf.
If I stand up on this footstool,
I can reach them by myself.

Kk

K this is a keyhole,
and this shiny thing's a key.
The key fits in the keyhole
and unlocks the lock for me.

L this is my ladder,
and it helps me to climb high.
I need to change these light bulbs.
Can you guess the reason why?

L l

LANCE
THE
WONDER
HORSE

LANCE
THE
WONDER
HORSE

Mm

M my name is Mumford,
and this is a magic trick.
I will now change this mud to milk.
It didn't work? Oh, ick!

Nn

N it is my nap time,
so I'm going to my nest.
I've played so hard all morning
that I need to take a rest.

Oo

O I am an ostrich.
I am so tall and grand.
When I want to hide myself
my head goes in the sand.

Pp

INK

20 19 18 17 16 15 14 13 12 11 10 9 8 7 6 5 4 3 2 1

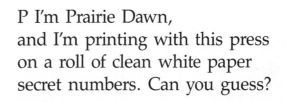

P I'm Prairie Dawn,
and I'm printing with this press
on a roll of clean white paper
secret numbers. Can you guess?

Qq

Q this is my quilt,
and I keep it on my bed.
It makes me feel quite snuggy
from my toes up to my head.

Rr

R I'm Rodeo Rosie,
and I love to play outside
on the ranch where I was reared
and learned to rope and ride.

Ss

S these are my seashells,
and I found them at the shore.
I love to sit and count them.
Splendid! Nothing thrills me more!

Tt

T this is a train,
and it runs upon a track.
Its whistle goes *woo-woo-woo*
and its wheels go *clicky-clack*.

Uu

U my new umbrella
is so good. Do you know why?
It's big enough to keep
all my friends completely dry.

V v

V for valentines to make,
and when you are all through,
the fun is giving them away.
I made one just for you!

I LOVE YOU!

W w

W for wagon,
it's a thing with wheels you pull.
It is easy when it's empty,
but it's harder when it's full.

Xx

X this is an x-ray—
a look at what's inside.
When you have an x-ray taken,
there is little you can hide.

Y this is a yo-yo,
and it is my favorite thing,
except that every time I try it,
I get tangled in the string.

Yy

Zz

Z this is a zebra—
if you said so, you were right.
Are the white stripes on the black,
or the black stripes on the white?

Now you know the alphabet—
the letters A to Z.
If you want to say it all again,
go back to A with me.